Just Believe

Stories of Inspiration

Rosemarie Monaco

ISBN-13: 978-1500883270
ISBN-10: 1500883271

Design by Rosemarie Monaco of Group M Inc www.groupm.org

Acknowledgements

There are so many who I need to acknowledge for making *Just Believe* a reality. I will list them here but I also want to acknowledge those who inspired my stories. Thank you for those precious sparks of light.

To my fellow authors, Angela Artemis and Sue Reif who encouraged me to put my stories together and who guided me through the process.

My dear friend Maria and my awesome sister, Tana— these are the two who nagged the loudest about turning my stories into a volume.

Then there is my soul sister, Lorraine who is always so proud of me. Her excitement over my work is forever exhilarating.

Growing up, my brother and I were not very close. After my mother died, that changed—she was the bond that brought us together. I'm certain it was part of her grand scheme. Since then he has been my anchor. I am so grateful for his faith in me.

I cannot say enough about Bill. His love and support keeps me alive, gives me wings, as one of my stories tells. He encouraged me to write this book in a way that made it all seem so easy. And it was. Thank you, my darling.

Just Believe

Rosemarie Monaco

Dedication

To Rose Giulia Della Valle Monaco,
ever, the most remarkable mother

Just Believe

Stories of Inspiration

Rosemarie Monaco

Table of Contents

Just Believe

Rosemarie Monaco

Introduction

My mother loved everything I created, ever since I was a little girl. Of course what mother does not love those unique, little presents that came from the heart of her child. But my mom, a creative herself, loved the very idea of creation—of making something where nothing was before—of creating something from an idea or a vision, of giving birth to something that was inside of you.

Even when I was an adult and could afford to buy her lovely trinkets or send her off on a vacation, much as she appreciated such gifts, they did not elicit the glow and deep satisfaction that something I made for her did. I used to think that she preferred my handmade gifts because she didn't want me to spend my money frivolously. She didn't feel the need, like most women do, to have fancy clothes or jewelry. She wanted me to save my money; to, in her mind, put it to better use.

Later on I realized that was only a very small part of it. She believed that I could do anything; that my handmade treasures were just that, treasures—a part of me that connected with her on a level so visceral that no store-bought gift could ever compare. I understood.

From then on for each birthday or holiday I would write her a poem, make her a card, frame a work of art. It made her so happy.

I decided to trust her judgment. Maybe I am as talented as she thinks; it's not just a mother's love that appreciates my work. So I gave it a try. By then I was the principal of a public relations agency and a professional writer. Instead of sending clients the usual bottle of wine or basket of goodies, I decided to make something instead. That was Christmas 2000. I wonder if there is significance in my beginning at the turn of a new century. Yes, I'm certain there is.

Introduction

At first I crafted holiday ornaments that I accompanied with a poem. But then my poems evolved into stories and took on a life of their own. Soon the stories themselves became the ornaments as I printed them on luscious paper and bound them by hand with tassels, bows and wire hangers. Still, I always included an ornament. Sometimes a beautiful ornament would inspire the story; other years it worked the other way around.

Clients, family and friends would tell me they couldn't wait to get my new story each year. What a wonderful compliment. My mother was right.

I wrote each story with the spirit of the child in mind. Pablo Picasso said "Every child is an artist. The problem is how to remain an artist once we grow up." That idea has always haunted me. What happens to us? Why do we banish the artist? Why do we stop believing in magic? Why did I not believe my mother?

My goal was to awaken the child in all of us; to return us to a place where anything is possible. Where all you have to do is dream to make it so. Because magic, you see, does exist. It's the inner power to make your dreams come true.

2000

The Gift

Outside my office doors is a deck surrounded by beautiful, plush trees, often the source of my inspiration. In the fall of 2000, I was working, when something made me look up. An oak leaf lilted across the glass door in slow motion, like a prima ballerina demanding my attention. I couldn't resist its alluring dance. I went outside and picked it up just as it landed. It was perfect, not a mark, just the rich patterns of its altering colors. I looked around. There were dozens just like it snuggled against their equally beautiful maple cousins. I began to collect them and brought them inside. I placed them inside the pages of my book collection to keep them from withering. How appropriate, I thought that these beautiful specimens get to spend time with William Shakespeare and Umberto Eco…as well as Michael Crichton and Stephen King. I knew I had to preserve them. And share their beauty. I adorned them with holiday glitter and colorful ribbons. They would be the first of my yearly holiday ornaments.

Following is the poem I wrote to accompany the embellished leaves.

Just Believe

Rosemarie Monaco

The Gift

Outside my door lives a tree.
This precious gift it gave to me.
Its beauty made me sad.

I thought...
how seasons...come and go.
No time to see them pass.

I thought...
The selfless tree,
It gave a part of it to me.

Then I knew why.

I thought...
of friends...of family,
of those I seldom see.

Inside my heart they live.
A precious gift they give.
Their beauty makes me glad.

Just Believe

Rosemarie Monaco

2001

The Pinecone

After receiving so many amazing responses in 2000, I knew I was on to something. What will I do in 2001?

I was walking my dogs in a beautiful park, nearby my home, on a path lined with a variety of majestic evergreen trees. I noticed a cluster of freshly fallen pinecones basking in the sunlight. I picked one up and knew. This was my next holiday ornament. I collected dozens of pinecones. I painted them, added beads, glitter and delicate ribbons. Each was unique.

I thought about how children see things that adults do not and that how all we have to do is look at life from their perspective to see the magic it holds. I wrote the following poem to accompany the pinecone ornaments.

Just Believe

Rosemarie Monaco

The Pinecone

"This is a magic pinecone," said the child.

"How could a pinecone be magic?" said the man.

"Well, if you look very close you will see."

"All I see are bristly brown petals."

"Bring it here into the light, then you'll see."

"Well it does sparkle in the light," said the woman, "but that doesn't mean it's magic."

"No, you just can't see from where you are," said the child.

"Let me show you. Right here, behind these petals are all your most beautiful memories. These others reflect all your greatest strengths. And these, the ones in the palm of your hand, hold all your dreams."

"But how does it work, the magic?" said the man.

"Well every time you put the cone in the light you will see all the things it holds. And know that all of them are right here within your reach."

"Look," said the woman, "look how beautiful it is in this light, just like the child said."

"Where ever did you find it?" said the man.

"I didn't," the child answered. "It was right here all along."

Just Believe

Rosemarie Monaco

2002

Tribute to 9-11

September 11, 2001 was a day few of us will ever forget. It continues to sting years later. The Christmas after the first anniversary of 9-11, I felt a burning need to honor the memory of the victims and the tragedy of sudden loss. I also wanted to impress upon us all how those who lost their lives live on—in us all. And how the spirit of the child helps us to heal.

With this story I included miniature snow-globe ornaments.

Just Believe

Rosemarie Monaco

A Tribute

Things just weren't the same since Daddy went away. Mom tried so hard, for her sake. She knew that. But even when Mommy laughed, it was different, thought Vanessa. Something about her eyes, they'd be looking right at her but seeing something else. Searching.

Nighttime was always the worst. Vanessa remembered how Daddy used to look in on her every night after she fell asleep. He told her he did that so he could watch her dream. And this way he could chase away all the bad dreams and make sure all the good ones came true. Falling asleep wasn't so easy now.

Vanessa rolled onto her side. Big, sparkling flakes drew her to the window. Mesmerized by their delicate beauty, she imagined that each and every flake was woven out of diamond dust by snow angels. "They tickle my eyes just to look at them," she thought. Her tears dry now, she smiled.

"If only I could catch them. I would put them in a jar. Then every time Mommy was sad I would open the jar and it would snow for us—beautiful tickly flakes. There must be a way."

She remembered her early-warning monster alarm— a glass jar holding pennies and other noise makers that she kept under her bed. Although it had been a very effective deterrent, it was definitely worth sacrificing if it would make Mommy happy again.

She reached under the bed and slid it out ever so carefully. She emptied the contents into one of her big plush slippers. Quickly she slipped on her pants, then her shoes. She put three layers of sweaters on with the hooded one Daddy gave her on top. She reached to unlatch the window. Using all her strength she pushed it open and jumped onto the soft white cushion below.

She nestled the uncovered jar into the softness. It was very important to capture only fresh snow. Already-fallen snow would not work. As the snow accumulated inside the jar, she lay back on the fallen blanket and let the flakes kiss her face. "I wonder if Daddy misses me?" she thought. "I wonder if it snows where he is?"

It would be best to leave the jar and get it in the morning. This way it would remain untouched as long as possible.

Vanessa made her way back through the window. She shed her wet clothes, and slid back into bed. Tomorrow everything would be better, she thought, as she fell off to sleep.

"Good morning, sleepy head. It's your lucky day," she heard her mother say. It snowed so hard during the night that there would be no school today.

Vanessa jumped out of bed and headed straight for the window. But it was gone. The snow was gone and so was the jar!

"What happened to the snow," she begged her mother.

"The snow plows came during the night, sweetheart, and took it away. And it's a good thing. We wouldn't have been able to get out the front door."

"But my jar. They took the jar."

"What jar? Whatever are you talking about, Nessa? Come on, let's go have something to eat and you and I will go build a snowman, what do you say?

"Thanks, Mom. But I'm not hungry."

"Are you sure, honey? It's nearly lunch time."

"I'm sure," said Vanessa through a resounding sneeze.

"Oh dear, maybe you'd better stay right where you are. I'll be right back."

The doorbell woke Vanessa up from a deep medicine-induced sleep.

"But I don't understand," she heard her mother say.

"Well, Ma'am it seems that this got moved around from one post office to another, what with all the confusion," the man said.

"But that was over a year ago."

"Yes, Ma'am, and we're terribly sorry. But between what happened that day and what followed…it got lost. Apparently, at one point, it fell off a conveyer belt and got stuck behind a table. Someone spotted it in the main post office last night and we just got it this afternoon. Considering the circumstances, we thought to get it to you as soon as possible."

"I see. Thank you."

Mommy looked like she saw a ghost, thought Vanessa, as her mother entered her room.

"What's that, Mommy?"

"It's a package. From Daddy. It's addressed to you."

Really? Oh, Mommy. Can I open it?"

"Well, yes. I guess so. It's yours."

Barely catching her breath, Vanessa pulled at the package. Inside was another box and two letters. One addressed to her and another for Mom.

"*My Sweet Ness…*

This is a reminder that no matter how far away I go, I'll always be right there with you, making sure all your dreams come true.

Love, Daddy

P.S. Take care of Mommy for me.

Hi Hon…

I know what you're thinking. I spoil her. But I saw this in D.C. and couldn't resist. And since I'm going directly to the airport from my meeting tomorrow morning in New York City, I thought I'd drop it in the mail. Wish I could be there to see her face. And yours. But I will be there... holding you while you dream.

Love forever, Ian

"Look Mommy, look at what Daddy sent me. You shake it and it snows inside. Isn't it beautiful?"

"It's the most beautiful thing I've ever seen, sweetheart."

How happy Mommy looks, Vanessa thought, even through her tears.

"Mommy, does this mean it snows in heaven?"

"Yes, my Sweet, I suppose it does."

Mother and daughter fell into a peaceful sleep that would last all through the night for the first time in more than a year.

A tribute to children everywhere whose courage and imagination give us hope.

2003

STAR BRIGHT

I always believed in the Law of Attraction, long before I knew it had a name. Even as a girl, I felt that there was something extraordinary I was meant to do. I just didn't know what, nor did I have a clue how I would go about doing it. You see, what I was really experiencing was the feeling that we can do or have, or make happen whatever we desire. I didn't know then that you have to recognize and nurture those desires and battle the goblins who would see you fail. Life had to teach me that.

Somewhere along the line, like most of us, I lost sight of that feeling. I stopped believing in magic. My mom used to tell that I could to anything I set my mind to. I loved her blind faith in me. But that is just what that was, I thought—blind. I know now what she meant.

Magic is everywhere; we just have to trust in it and allow it to do its work. We have to believe in the "light"—call it intuition, inspiration, knowledge, the power of the universe, whatever you will. It will guide us home or allow us to find a new path. All we have to do is ask.

I found sparkling, metallic stars to go with this story. I delivered them in an organza pouch—to capture their glittering magic.

Just Believe

Rosemarie Monaco

STAR BRIGHT

"I wish I may, I wish I might. Daddy? Where did that come from? The star wish, you know, star light, star bright?" said Melissa.

"Ahhh, well. It's an old Indian legend," said Dad.

"Indian legend?"

"Yes, there was this tribe. A secret Indian tribe that used to live in the mountains."

"What do you mean, it was secret?"

"Well, nobody knew about them, not even other Indians. And they were mystical.

"Mystical?"

"Yes, they had powers. They had a special connection with the stars. They could make things happen."

"Like what, Daddy?"

"Mmmm, well, they could make it rain when the crops were thirsty. And cause the maple trees to laugh until they cried sweet, delicious tears."

"Tell, me Daddy! Tell me more!" Melissa said, giggling.

"OK. I'll tell you the whole starry story."

Once upon a...star, there was an Indian tribe called the, um...the Stella Indians. Yes, Stella for star. Some say they got their name and powers because they lived so high up in the mountains they could actually touch the stars.

"Uhh, wow! But, Daddy, if the Indian tribe was secret, how did anyone find out about them?"

"Well, that's all part of the story. Just listen and I'll tell you."

It was a cold December day, a long, long time ago. The Simons were on the way to visit their grandma for the holiday. There was Mr. and Mrs. Simon, Tina, and Timmy, the youngest. He was just about your age, in fact.

The family was very tired after traveling all day and set up camp right at the base of the mountain where the Stella Indians lived. Back then, there were no cars, so people traveled by horse-drawn wagon, and it was much too dangerous to travel after dark.

After dinner, Mr. Simon made warm, cozy sleeping bags from the quilts and blankets that were in the back of the wagon. The whole family gathered round the fire. They sang songs and talked about how warm and happy it would be at grandma's house, especially this time of year when families and friends everywhere give little gifts to show how much they love each other.

It was a beautiful night. The stars were so bright! Mom and Dad fell asleep right away. But Tina and Timmy couldn't sleep. They were mesmerized by the stars.

"Mezmerimes?"

Mez-mer-ized. It's a little like being hypnotized. It's when something captures your attention and you just can't look away.

Tina and Timmy couldn't take their eyes off the stars. They talked and talked, and looked for animal shapes among the stars. Eventually Tina fell off to sleep. But not Timmy. He had never seen stars like these, the way they twinkled. One star was so bright it lit up a nearby cloud making it look like a mound of vanilla frosting just floating in the darkness.

He got up and wandered over to the hillside. He saw these big boulders and decided to climb on top of them to get closer to the stars. But then once he did, he wanted to get even closer. He climbed and climbed keeping his eyes on the stars. Suddenly, he stumbled and fell. He hit his head. Not seriously, but he was dazed, just enough to lose his bearings, his sense of direction. He didn't know where he was. He kept wandering thinking he was still going up, but he wasn't anymore. Instead he was moving deep into the mountain.

"Wasn't he scared, Daddy?"

"Well, he wasn't scared at first, not exactly. But he knew something was wrong. Don't forget, honey, things were different back then. It was frontier times. Boys and girls had to learn to take care of themselves when they were very young. They learned to be very brave.

"OK, now where was I? Oh yes."

He was walking farther into the mountain. Then he saw something in the clearing up ahead. He couldn't quite make it out but it was sparkling, like glitter. Probably from the moonlight, he thought.

As he came closer he could see that there were people—Indians clustered around the twinkling spot. They were chanting something in low whisper-like voices.

Suddenly they stopped. There was dead silence. Timmy heard one man say something, but he couldn't understand the words. The man sounded concerned, troubled about something. One of the women turned around and saw Timmy.

"A boy!" she said. "Over there."

Timmy turned to run away. A wall of Indians stood in his way; their arms folded in defiance. They stared at Timmy giving him a fierce look. Timmy froze. He didn't know what to do.

Then a man with a big colorful headdress said, "We can't let him go. He'll tell about us. Our culture, our way of life will be ruined!"

Timmy didn't understand any of the words. But he knew. Somehow he knew exactly what they were saying. And now; now, he was terrified.

"Uhhhhh," gasped Melissa.

Down at the Simon's campsite, Mrs. Simon woke from her sleep as if someone had shaken her. Her heart was pounding. She knew something was wrong. She ran to check on the children. Tina was still sleeping, but Timmy was nowhere in sight.

She looked everywhere frantically. Then on the side of the hill, near the boulders she saw Timmy's night cap. She ran back to wake Mr. Simon.

"Thomas, Thomas! Timmy is gone," she shouted. "I think he climbed the mountain!"

"Be still Liza. He probably just wandered off. You know how curious and restless he can be."

"He isn't here, I tell you. He's gone," she answered.

Mr. Simon searched everywhere. He knew she was right. Timmy was in danger."

At daybreak, Tina woke and asked for Timmy.

"He's gone! Into the mountains! Didn't you see him leave? Why didn't you watch him? You were supposed to take care of him?" Mrs. Simon shouted.

Tina trembled. Mrs. Simon threw her arms around Tina and pulled her tight, crying. "I'm sorry sweetheart. It isn't your fault. I'm so sorry."

"It's ok Mommy. I can climb up the rocks. I'll go after him. He can't be too far," said Tina.

"No, I can't let you go. It's too dangerous. Your father will go. You and I need to stay here in case Timmy comes back."

"But what happened to Timmy, Daddy?" said Melissa.

"I'm getting there."

Through his fear, Timmy wished with all his might to be back with his family. Then he saw that light again. It got brighter, then weaker, just like a twinkling star, he thought. But this was here on earth, right in front of him.

Then, from where Timmy had seen the light came a little girl. She walked over to Timmy then turned to face the Indians.

"This little boy is lost. His family is looking for him. They are so very, very sad. We must return him to his family. If we don't, we will cause a pain so deep it will put a hole in the sky and all the stars will vanish forever!"

"Then you will have to guide him, Stella, said the chief to the girl." She took Timmy by the hand. "Come with me," she said. "I'll take you home."

Back down at the Simon's campsite Mrs. Simon and Tina packed up the wagon while they waited for Mr. Simon to return. Daytime slowly faded into night. When Mr. Simon arrived alone, Mrs. Simon screamed her son's name in agony, "Timmy!"

Mr. Simon held her close. "We'll keep looking," Liza. We'll go get help and keep looking. But Mrs. Simon knew that there was little chance of finding Timmy alive in the wilds of the mountain land.

She looked up at the sky. Once again the stars were shining

brightly. "Oh heavenly star so bright, please light the way back home for my Timmy," she prayed.

She walked over to where she found Timmy's cap. Through her tears she saw an unusual light coming through the trees. She thought it was her imagination. Then it moved ever so soft and gently, like a veiled candle light. As it came closer it got brighter and brighter, twinkling through the leaves. Then it faded as suddenly as it appeared. In its place she saw Timmy.

"Timmy, Timmy! cried Mrs. Simon. Mr. Simon and Tina came running over. They couldn't believe their eyes. There he was, perfectly fine.

"Where were you? What happened?" said Mr. Simon.

"I got lost. But Stella showed me the way?

"Stella, who's Stella?"

"The Indian girl from the mountain."

"What Indian girl? What are you talking about? There are no Indians here in this part of the country. It's not possible."

"She's right here, see?"

"Sweetheart, there's no one there." Timmy looked around. But she was just there! He was holding her hand. Where did she go?

"What's that you have in your hand, Timmy? said Mrs. Simon.

Timmy opened up his hand. There it was. The brightest star they'd ever seen. Timmy and his Mom gasped with astonishment. This was the light that guided him home.

"So Daddy, did Stella and the Indians really exist?"

"No one really knows. Some say Timmy just dreamed it all. Others believe that his desire was so strong that he created them, and the light.

What do you think? Melissa."

2004

The Light

The theme of "seeing the light" returned to my consciousness in 2004, with a bit of a twist. The media showered us with dozens of stories about racist attacks. Only the players were different. Since 9-11, Muslims were the new targets of our irrational hatred. Yes, our 9-11 attackers were Muslim, but it was Al Qaida who attacked us, not our Muslim neighbors. It got me thinking about how prejudice begins. Kids, after all, do not see color, or religion or gender. To them everyone is equal. They learn hatred from their parents—and the media. I wanted to write a story about how, while each of us is different, we are all connected regardless of origin; how ultimately we need each other; and that if we learn the importance of cooperation, maybe, just maybe we can eradicate hatred.

With each story I included a holiday candle, hoping to shed some light, symbolically and literally.

Just Believe

Rosemarie Monaco

The Light

Sammy walked into the recreation room. His crimson nose and icy moustache told how cold the late afternoon was long before he spoke. "Better bundle up little ladies and gents. We're ready to roll."

"I wish the snow would let up some," said Mrs. Thompson.

"Don't worry, Mrs. T, I took the service road on the last trip back. It's pretty clean," said Sammy. "I'm almost glad the bus had to be serviced. I'd rather be driving the SUV, even if it means a few extra trips. It's so much safer in any weather."

"Well, OK. You'd better get going. Come on children."

This year's holiday trip was going to be so special. The third-grade class talked of nothing else for weeks. When they arrived at Winter Village they'd find a wonderland. Peppermint trees made up entirely of little candy canes ready to be picked, giant coconut snowmen and chocolate-covered cookie reindeer. And Maestro the Magician would make toys appear out of thin air. They'd even heard about the mysterious orphan girl who had special powers, or so they said. According to some of the villagers, at night she would cast a glow so warm and bright it could melt snow. Her light, they say, is a beacon that leads you to secret treasures.

Are all five children on board?" called Sammy. "Say 'snowman' as I call your name.

Jason Marks?"

"Snowman"

"Sue Li?"

"Snowman"

"Calvin Little"

"Snowman"

"Aaron Haneef?"

"Snowman"

"Angela Stewart?"

"SnowGIRL"

"That you are!"

"We're on our way," said Sammy followed by a chorus of "Yeh!"

Halfway to the Winter Village, what the weatherman said would be light snow was looking more like a light blizzard. Sammy wasn't too worried. He was confident that his Jeep could handle anything. The jumble of little voices assured him that the children were completely unaware of what was going on outside the car. Just as well, he thought.

What startled him was a sudden howl of wind. The trees began to sway. The snow fell in furious swirls. Before he could utter a word, a huge tree limb, as if from nowhere, smashed the windshield. Like a baseball bat slamming a toy car, it threw the Jeep over on its side, skidding across the road into snow-lit bushes.

Jason pushed the side-door handle opening it up to the sprinkling night sky. He climbed out. Next came Sue. One at a time the other children managed their way out. Remarkably not one of them was hurt.

"Where's Sammy?" said Sue.

"He's just over there. He must have gone through the windshield," said Jason. "Oh Boy, he's not moving. There's blood on his head. What'll we do?"

"Let me see," said Sue. "Oh my gosh. Is he dead?"

"No, he's breathing."

"Well, look in his pocket, he must have a cell," shouted Angela.

"Oh no! Look at this," cried Calvin as he displayed the mangled phone he retrieved from under the fallen SUV. "What'll we do now?"

"Look there's a light, back behind the trees," said Sue. "It moved. There it is again."

"There's nothing out there," said Jason. "It's probably a reflection."

"I don't see a light but I do see a house," said Aaron.

"I don't see anything," said Jason. "You're hallucinating."

"He's right," said Angela. "Look, through the bushes."

"OK, let's you and me go check it out, Calvin. Aaron, you stay here with the girls."

"I spotted it. I'll go. You can stay here with the girls."

"Hey guys, don't sweat it," said Calvin. "You two go. I'll stay here."

"No, I'm not going with him."

"Hey, I'll go with Aaron," said Angela. "You stay here with the girls."

"Ha, Ha, Ha," responded Calvin.

"Wait, my Dad always has a flashlight in his car. Maybe Sammy has one too." Angela looked into the front of the SUV. The glove compartment was hanging open. "I don't see anything."

"Let me see," said Sue as she wiggled her slim body into the front passenger seat. "There it is, on the floor. I think I can reach it."

"Ok, now listen up," said Jason. "Ange, you take the flashlight. "I'll stay here. Sue, Calvin you get back into the car, use the blanket Sammy gave us if you get cold. I'll wait out here in case Sammy wakes up."

It wasn't long before Aaron and Angela came running back. "It's not far. It's an old cabin. We can stay there."

"What are we going to do about Sammy?" asked Calvin. "We can't just leave him here, he'll freeze."

Sue turned. "What's that? Over there!"

"I don't see anything," said Jason. "What are you talking about?"

"It's a light, over there. It moved. Someone's there!"

"There's nothing there."

"Look let's just figure out what we're going to do about Sammy."

"I know," said Angela. "Last month me and my mom moved the piano, just the two of us. She lifted a leg at a time and I put a rug under it. Then all we had to do was drag the rug and the piano came with it."

"Yeah well where are we gonna get a rug out here," snapped Calvin.

"We don't need one," said Aaron. "We have the blanket. Angela is right, we can do it."

Sue pulled the blanket out of the fallen Jeep. As Jason and Calvin lifted Sammy's shoulders, Sue and Angela placed the blanket underneath him. The two boys, one on either side of Sammy were able to lift his bottom just enough for Angela to pull the blanket under and down. Now, with the heaviest part of his body supported by the blanket, they were able to drag Sammy through the freshly fallen snow with ease. It was like giving Sammy a sleigh ride, remarked Sue.

When they reached the cabin Angela stopped short. "Oh great. Now what? How are we going to get him up the steps?"

"Look, there it is again. The light," said Sue.

"She's right. I saw something too," said Aaron.

"Oh great. Now they are both seeing things. Maybe its Allah and Buddha lighting the way," said Jason.

"And maybe you're too blind to see anything," said Aaron.

"I see you. I see bad news. My dad told me never to trust someone like you."

"Hey, shut up, Jason. You think you know everything," said Angela.

"I know there isn't a light and we have a problem."

"Look, over there." Sue pointed to a thin plank of wood leaning against the house.

"Hey, that wasn't there before," said Angela. "We came right by here."

"Well, it's here now," said Jason shaking his head in disbelief. It figures, he thought, he shouldn't have trusted Aaron and Angela in the first place.

"OK. All we have to do is put it over the steps and we can slide Sammy right up."

Sammy and the children were safely in the cabin now. But their only light came from the flashlight that had guided them all this way. It was beginning to fade.

Sue began to cry. "What are we going to do?" We have no heat, the flashlight is dying and we have no way to get help."

"We'll be okay," said Jason, "When the daylight comes we can find our way out easily. And we'll get help."

"For your information, in this weather we could all freeze to death long before morning. And what about Sammy. Maybe he'll be dead by morning," shouted Calvin.

Sue shivered. Her tears were uncontrollable.

"Now look what you've done," said Angela.

"Look, there it is again. The light. Look, right outside the window."

"This time Calvin saw the light too. He walked over to the window but he couldn't make it out. "It's like a candlelight, flickering," he said.

"I am now convinced that you're all going nuts," strained Jason.

"Maybe it's you," insisted Angela. "You're the only one who doesn't see the light."

"Look at this, look at what I found," said Aaron. "There's a pot on the stove. It wasn't here before. I know it. And there's soup in it!"

"Let me see," said Jason. Sure enough, the pot was filled with wonderful smelling soup. Just like Mom's. Jason turned up the flame. The soup began to simmer. "There's got to be an explanation for this."

"And look, here in the cupboard. There are bowls and spoons, six of them," said Calvin.

"Whoa," said Jason. "He can count."

"It was the light. Don't you see?" said Sue. "Every time we see the light, something good happens."

"That's right!" said Angela. "We found the cabin after I saw the first light."

"And the wooden plank," added Sue. "And now the soup and the bowls."

"Yeah, well your magic light doesn't know how to count," said Jason. Because there are only five of us and six bowls."

"Listen," interrupted Aaron. There was a gentle knock at the door. And a faint voice. "Help. Help."

Calvin opened the door. A little girl stood on the doorstep. She was dressed all in white—white like the snow. Standing on the doorstep, with the snow surrounding her, all you could make out was her face illuminated by the candle she held in front of her. Her face glowed.

"May I come in," she said softly.

"Yes, of course."

"Where did you come from?" said Sue.

"Did you get lost in the storm too?" asked Angela.

"I am so happy I found you," said the girl. "May I have some soup?"

"Uhhh...the sixth bowl!" said Sue.

"OK, where did you come from?" asked Jason, still skeptical.

The girl smiled at him and said "You need to believe in your friends, Jason."

"How do you know my name?"

She smiled at him. "My name is Lucy." She turned toward Sammy. "I see your friend is hurt." The girl walked over to Sammy and put her candle down beside him.

Sammy stirred. "Where am I?" His groggy voice jolted the children.

"Sammy, Sammy," said Sue. "We were in an accident. Are you OK?"

"I think so, I'm just very sleepy."

"You'll be fine," said Lucy. "Just rest now. Everything will be alright." Sammy drifted off to sleep. "I think it would be best if we took his wet blanket out from under him."

As Calvin, Aaron and Angela removed the blanket, the wind howled. The windows rattled. The door burst open. The cold air whirled in.

The children tried to close the door, but the wind was too strong for them. They all huddled in the corner near Sammy, away from the icy wind.

"Look, I can see my breath. It's freezing," said Sue.

"We need to build a fire," said Lucy.

"How?" said Jason. "There's no wood in the fireplace. Or maybe one will magically appear."

"There are many ways to make a fire, Jason." Standing close to Sammy, Lucy closed her eyes. Her face glowed in the candlelight.

"My grandfather told me that in the desert, the nights can be as cold as the day is hot," said Aaron. "People huddle close together with a blanket around them. The bodies make heat and it is as warm as sitting by a fire."

"What a wonderful idea," said Lucy. The children gathered close to Sammy pulling the blanket around them. Before long, the warmth embraced the children like a mother's arms.

Jason got up. "I think one of us needs to do something." But it was so cold that as soon as Jason slipped out from behind the blanket a piercing chill rushed in.

"We need you," said Lucy.

"The more of us there are the greater the warmth," said Aaron.

The air was so cold it pinched Jason's face. He realized now that he too, needed them. He returned to the others. The warmth they generated cradled the children to sleep.

It's time now," said Lucy as she nudged Jason awake. She took the candle from beside Sammy and passed it to him. "Take the candle, it will light the way." Jason looked at Lucy and understood.

"Here," he said to Aaron. "You were right all along. You should be our guide." Aaron smiled at Jason, took the candle and simply placed it on the windowsill.

The sirens startled the children from a deep sleep. While paramedics tended to Sammy, moms and dads rushed to their children.

"How did you find us?" asked Angela.

"We found the Jeep, and then we saw the light," said her mom.

"I'm so proud of you," said Jason's dad.

"But it was Lucy. Lucy saved us."

"Lucy? Who's Lucy?

"The girl with the light."

"Son, there's no Lucy here. What saved you was keeping warm under the blanket. That was so smart. Was that you're idea, Jason?"

"No. It was Aaron's."

"Aaron?"

"Yes, sir," said Aaron. "But Jason is right. Lucy saved us."

"She has to be here," said Jason. Jason and Aaron ran outside to look for the girl. She was nowhere in sight.

"Lucy, with a light, you say?" asked Angela's mom. "It must have been a dream, dear. Don't you remember? When we were looking for names for your baby sister? Lucy means Light, sweetheart. It was just a dream."

The children stared at each other. Could it be? Was it just a dream? How could we all have had the same dream?

Dazed, wondering, yet feeling that Lucy really had been there, the children left with their parents.

When they arrived home, each of the children found something in their pockets. It was a candle with a note attached. It read:

Wherever we're from, whatever our name

The goodness inside is exactly the same.

Remember this, even when you're grown.

We're better together than we are alone.

Wherever you go, whatever you fear,

Kindle the flame and I will be there.

Remember this, whenever doubt sets in.

The power of the light comes from within.

-- Lucy

2005

The Faerie & The Mirror

Do I believe in faeries? Why yes, most certainly. They are helpers, imaginary or otherwise. They are the spirit that guides us. But what you see when this poem unfolds is that the courage we need to attain our goals already exists within us. So perhaps you could say that our faerie guide is the voice we hear inside. We just have to learn to listen.

You will also see that I did not ignore the fact that life is riddled with obstacles. Mostly, these are obstacles we create, for a variety of very sound reasons. Yet, as their creator, we can also eliminate them. We do that by focusing on our goals. If we believe in ourselves and trust our ability we can, as the cliché commands, move mountains…or in the case of this story, climb giant trees. We tend to look outside ourselves for answers, ignoring our own wisdom. With each poem I enclosed a mirror as a reminder that the answers lie within.

Just Believe

Rosemarie Monaco

The Faerie & The Mirror

I saw this tree. In the distance.
Tall and green and sparkling.
I couldn't resist it.

As I neared, its beauty revealed.
Toys and candy and red-bowed boxes
Dangled from its sugary branches.

Around the tree, a mired moat.
Where are we? In a long lost place?
Am I dreaming? No.

I heard a voice. A faerie's voice.
Half birdsong. Half human.
The most enchanting sound.

Do you love my tree? she sang.
I made it just for thee.
She giggled.

But why me?
Where is this place?
How did I get here?

Just Believe

So many questions.
You ought to know
You wished me so.

Her wings glistened.
In the sunlight
That scattered through the tree.

Her skin was shiny.
Iridescent.
So many beautiful colors.

I never wished for a tree.
Tough it is very lovely,
It is still a tree.

Oh no, not any tree.
This one knows just how
Dreams come true, you'll see.

But I can't get to it.
I'll never know what to do
To make my dreams come true.

Just Believe

Close your eyes.
See the tree.
It reaches out for thee.

Her faerie voice echoed,
Splitting every word
Into a hundred meanings.

Yes, I see. A limb reaching low.
But I'm much too afraid
I'll fall in the mire.

Focus on one thing,
I heard the faerie sing.
Embrace it. And believe.

A step is not a step
She spoke,
Unless a step you take.

I stretched my arm out far.
I took the limb. Held it close,
Looking only at its path.

Just Believe

You were so right,
I said gleefully.
I'm here beneath the tree.

One victory you see
Will bring you more,
If more you see.

I climbed and climbed
I saw a golden box, tied with a card
Open only if you're very smart.

Think of all you know,
The fairy said. Then know
What you don't know.

I know I can untie a knot.
And I'll do that right now.
But the box, it has no lid.

Now I see. It needs a key.
But I haven't one.
How can I open up the box?

Just Believe

If the key, you don't know,
The key will make you grow.
Knowing it is the key.

Her voice was like an angel's.
Her riddles made me think.
And then I knew what I needed to.

I looked past glistening leaves.
And there before my eyes
I saw a book for opening.

I read it through. Then I knew
Exactly what to do.
I opened up the box.

And there I found a note.
You're almost there, it read.
You can climb and reach the top.

I did it then. I looked way up.
I saw on top a sparkling light.
I climbed and climbed. I knew I could.

Just Believe

I reached and reached.
But then the light blinded me.
This was so much harder than before.

The faerie's voice I could not hear.
Then I remembered
What she whispered near to me.

Breathe deep the air. Then let it free.
Close your eyes. You will see.
All you need is inside of thee.

When in doubt, look at you.
See what makes dreams come true.
Atop the tree it will be.

I understood her sweet song now.
I closed my eyes. The light took shape.
I reached for it. It fell to me.

And in the silvery glass
I saw, looking back at me,
Everything I ever wanted to be.

Just Believe

I've climbed a thousand trees since then.
And found so many dreams. It's true.
And now I pass this on to you.

Let this mirror remind you well.
The magic is inside of you
It's you who makes your dreams come true.

Just Believe

Rosemarie Monaco

2006
In Search of an Angel

While this story is fictional, it is based on a real-life experience. I was about four years old. We lived in Brooklyn. My mom always took me shopping with her at what I remember to be a very crowded farmer's market on Fulton Street. She let go of my hand for just an instant and I twirled out of sight. No, I was not kidnapped, but I did meet an angel that day.

As I was looking for a familiar sight on the street that I had wandered to, a police officer approached me. I knew not to talk to strangers, but policemen were okay, mom told me that. He asked where my mother was and if I knew my address. I proudly recited "452 Columbia Street." He walked me home and there was my rather frantic mom in the square outside our apartment building. I ran to her. I don't remember the police officer after that. That memory reminded me that there are angels everywhere. They appear, unexpectedly, when we need them most.

As you might guess, my story was accompanied by a beautiful angel ornament.

Just Believe

Rosemarie Monaco

In Search of an Angel

"There's no such thing. Angels don't exist; those are just stories adults make up," said Michael.

"They do so exist," shouted Celia.

Just then, Celeste walked in. Michael and Celia loved Celeste. She came to stay with them every time Mom and Dad went out. She was so smart. She told them such wonderful stories. She just seemed to know everything.

"Hey guys, what's all the shouting about?"

"Michael says angels don't exist," said Celia.

"Oh I see," said Celeste.

"Tell her the truth, Celeste. Angels are just make-believe," insisted Michael.

"Well, it so happens, Michael, that angels do exist," answered Celeste. "I know because I met one."

"You did?" said Celia. "See, I knew it. Did she have wings? Was she beautiful?"

"Well, not exactly. Let me tell you my story…"

> It was just before my fifth birthday, so I was about your age, Celia. One day, right after dropping my brother off at school, my mother took me shopping with her and her girlfriend Grace. I loved going shopping with Mom. It made me feel like such a big girl. This day, the market was especially crowded. There were people everywhere.

Mom held my hand so tight. Being so little, all I could see were legs and skirts everywhere.

Grace asked Mom to help her with something and Mom let go of my hand for an instant. Everyone around me seemed to be moving so fast. I grabbed hold of Mom's skirt and instead of Mom, some strange lady looked down at me and said, "Let go little girl."

I looked around everywhere. Mom was nowhere to be seen. Just then a lady took me by the hand and said, "Come with me. I'll take you to your mother." I was so relieved. I mean, I was so scared. But now this lady was going to help me.

We walked a little bit, and then she led me to this car. I asked her why we were getting into a car. Mom was over there, in the other direction somewhere. "Don't worry sweetheart," she said. "Your Mom's friend had a little accident. She had to rush her to the hospital. She asked me to take care of you until she got back. My name is Demona. Don't you worry, now. I'll take good care of you."

I didn't like this woman much—there was just something about her. But her story made perfect sense. Mom never, ever left me alone before, but it would be just like her to help someone in need, especially her friend, Grace. And if she told this woman to mind me then I figured I ought to do as she asked.

We drove up to this house. It was very big, very pretty. It was blue with white trim and a big porch that wrapped all around the outside. It had lavender shutters and lace curtains on the windows. It looked like a house a princess would live in. I'd never seen anything like it. I couldn't wait to go inside.

When we got inside, Demona took me right to this room in the back of the house. She said this would be my very own room until Mom came to get me. She left and locked the door behind her.

When I turned to look around, I saw that the room was empty except for a cot with a blanket and a pillow on it. Nothing else. Well, Mom would be there soon, I thought, so it didn't matter.

I lay down on the cot and fell asleep. The next thing I heard was someone opening the door. It was Demona. She gave me a tray with a bowl of dry cereal and a glass of water. She said that was all she had, but that I had to eat it all up.

"When is my mother coming?" I asked. There's been a complication, she told me, so my mother wouldn't be coming for another day. This didn't seem right. Mom just wouldn't leave me like that. But then, maybe Grace really needed her and she thought I'd be okay.

Demona left the room, locked the door and didn't come back. I was scared, but I didn't know why. I cried and started to doze off again. I had lost all concept of time. The window in the room was locked and shuttered so I couldn't see outside. Next thing I knew, Demona came back and told me that I would have to help her clean the house.

"Now that I'm stuck with you, you'll have to earn your keep," she said.

All the shutters, all through the house were now closed, so I couldn't see outside from any of the rooms. She made me wash the floors, and dust all the furniture. I even had to scrub the walls!

Michael and Celia gasped. "Weren't you scared?" asked Celia.

"What did you do?" Michael wanted to know.

Yes, I was scared. With tears swelling in my eyes, I asked her where my mother was. "She's not coming. She may never come!" she shouted.

"No," I said. "No, that's a lie; my mother would never leave me."

"That's what you think sweetie. She wants to go out with her friends; she doesn't want to be tied down with a little brat like you."

"No, no," I shouted as I ran to my room. Demona followed me and locked the door behind me.

I cried myself to sleep again. A few hours later I woke up. I didn't know it then because I still couldn't see outside, but it must have been about 4:00 in the morning. I knew I had to find a way out. I had to get out of there and find my Mom. After several attempts, I was able to open the window but the shutters were locked so tight they wouldn't budge. That's when I saw a sliver of sunlight against the wall. I followed the ray of light with my eyes. It was coming through a crack in the shutters—as if the breaking day was reaching out to me.

I took the spoon from my cereal bowl and wedged it into the crack. At first, nothing, but then surprisingly, it cracked open and the entire slat fell off. I was so scared it would wake someone. I held my breath, then pushed and pushed until another slat broke loose. This time I stopped it from falling. The wood must have been old, because the next few slats came off easily until I had removed enough of them to slip my whole body through.

It was a little bit of a fall to the ground below, but I thought taking a chance would be better than staying with Demona. Luckily, the ground below was soft. I got up and ran as far away from that house, as fast as I could.

I had no idea where I was. I wandered and wandered. But I was still afraid that Demona would find me. Then out of nowhere, this lady appeared. She walked up to me and asked me if I needed help. I was afraid though. After all, the last person who wanted to help me was Demona. But as I looked up right behind her there was this glow. And it got brighter and brighter.

"What did she look like?" asked Celia.

Not anything like you might imagine. She was dark. She had dark hair and deep brown eyes. Her skin was a deep olive color. She looked like an ordinary person from the neighborhood. Even though I was still afraid, when she smiled at me somehow I knew she was there to help me. She took me into a café and got me some hot chocolate and a muffin. I told her everything that had happened. She walked over to the man behind the counter. They talked for a few minutes. He looked at me and nodded and picked up his phone. Then she came back to get me and we left.

I didn't understand how she knew where to take me, but before I knew it I was on the street where I lived. Standing in front of our apartment building in the same dress she wore when I saw her last was my Mom. We ran to each other. She took me in her arms and squeezed me so tight she nearly took my breath away. We both cried and cried and hugged. The lady was just standing there, smiling so big and wide. My Mom thanked her for all she had done.

She came over to me and knelt down by my side and said, "you're safe now, no one can harm you."

"Who are you?" I asked.

"My name is Gabriella," she said with this big glorious smile. "Go to your mother now."

I turned to my Mom and I asked her if she knew Gabriella. "Who is she Mom?" I said. "She's our special angel, my love, the angel who brought you back to me."

When I turned back to Gabriella to thank her and say goodbye, she was gone. She had just vanished.

"Wow," said Michael. "But what ever happened to Demona?"

Later on, Mom told me that the police had come and arrested her. So she could never harm me or any other little girl again.

So you see, angels don't always look like you see them in pictures. They can look like ordinary people. But what makes them different… and so very special…is that they are filled with goodness—from head to toe. And whatever your journey, wherever you're headed, if you believe in yourself, when you feel lost, your angel will be there to help you the rest of the way. Just like mine did.

2007

Imagination is the beginning of Creation
– George Bernard Shaw

I love Shaw's quote. I also believe that whatever we can imagine we can create. I used to write inspirational speeches for corporate executives. My research led me to scientific studies and interviews with successful business leaders and athletes. All the data I collected revealed a common pattern—those who succeed, whether they were aware of it or not, used the amazing power of visualization. Stars such as Michael Jordan would see the shot in his mind right before he nailed it. Michael Phelps visualized the perfect swim before he went to sleep each night. Albert Einstein relied on imagination too. "Logic will get you from A to B. Imagination will take you everywhere," he said.

I wanted this story to do three things—put us back in touch with the vivid imagination of our child selves, demonstrate that by using your mind's eye you can see so much and illustrate that you can indeed create what you imagine.

The ornament I included with my story was an embellished bird. I sprinkled the inner packaging with feathers.

Just Believe

Rosemarie Monaco

Imagination is the beginning of Creation

I started flying when I was four. I would go to the top of the hill, spread my wings way out far and they would lift me off the ground.

I flew so effortlessly, like a bird. No, better than a bird. More powerful, but just as agile. That's probably because my wings were made of velvet. Midnight blue. They were feathered with magenta lace and turquoise chiffon. This combination allowed me to float from tree to tree or soar way up high.

Most days I didn't fly very high. I preferred to stay close enough so I could see the fields of deep purple plums, crimson red cherries and sweet golden apricots. I imagined an emperor's rich green robe embroidered with rubies and garnets and glistening gold beads.

I made friends with a bluejay. His name was Byron. He loved the fruit trees. He invited me into his little house. But it was little only from the outside with its roof of twigs molded with mud. But when you went inside, it was enormous. The walls were papered with amber leaves. Holly berries draped the windows. There was a thick plush rug made of moss. And a pebbled stairway. Byron and I told each other stories. Sometimes we'd laugh so hard we'd just fall asleep on the bed made of freshly wormed silvery silk.

The best part about flying was how free and lighthearted it made me feel, which was especially fine after a difficult day. I knew in my heart that I would always be able to fly. Because when I did, I understood so much. I could see the truth. Watch every act unfold, every day. And there in the middle of life I'd see an answer.

One of my favorite things was hopping clouds. You have to be very careful though. They look soft and cushiony, but they are really very slippery. Yet, they feel so good. A warm quenching mist soothing your skin. Sometimes it tickled.

You might think it difficult to fly at night. It isn't at all. All you need is a crescent moon to light the sky. Otherwise grab hold of a star. Don't worry about burning your fingers. They aren't all that hot. They are more like mirrors than flames. They catch moonlight. And fill with angel dust. That's what makes them twinkle. I did carry a compass with me though. That North Star can be very unreliable.

Adults always told me I needed to have my feet planted firmly on the ground. How silly is that? I thought. I'm not a tree. That is not to say trees aren't nice. They are extraordinary individuals who know a thing or two.

I learned so much from flying so young. It got harder as I got older. But every time the world around me tried to keep me down, I remembered the advice of a great golden oak. He said that nothing can ever tether your imagination. Your mind can take you anywhere.

"I've got to run now, my love. I have to make my flight."

"But Mommy, the plane can't leave without the pilot."

"I know, honey. But it wouldn't be very nice of me to keep all those people waiting."

2008

Believe

It's such a shame that adults take Santa Claus away from us. How magical it was to see those presents appear under the tree on Christmas morning. Yes, I know someone put them there. But I also know that if you take away that spark, the spark that allows us to believe that we can make dreams come true, then we stop trying.

While I wrote my stories at Christmastime, I was careful not to attach any religious leaning to them. Christians, Jews and people of other faiths have gift-giving holidays around the same time of year. My stories are for everyone. They are about the common spirit, the god that is within all of us, if you will, and not about any religion. But this year, I wanted to write a story about the power of belief and I could not think of a better metaphor than Santa Claus. For my Jewish friends along with the Santa ornament, I included a little research that lightheartedly proved that Santa was part Jewish. I have included it here.

An aside…When I first moved into my home in the Hudson Valley, I named the beautiful oak tree, the giver of my inspiration for my first holiday story, Oliver.

Just Believe

Rosemarie Monaco

Believe

How are you today, Oliver?

Why I'm just fine, little one. I was just enjoying the crisp winter air flowing through my branches. But I say, you look a little sad, Miss Amy. Has something happened?

The kids at school said there is no such thing as Santa Claus. That he is just a fairytale parents tell their little kids. And that I'm a baby for believing.

Oh dear, my goodness gracious, that's very serious. Have you asked your parents about this?

Yeah. Mom says now that I'm seven, I'm pretty grown up and it's time I knew the truth. She says Santa is make-believe. All these years I believed. It was all a lie!

Oh dear child, you mustn't say that! Anything wonderful, that brings joy and happiness isn't a lie. Why, that just goes against the laws of the universe.

What do you mean?

Well, everything that is real starts with believing. If you want to be a dancer, first you have to believe that you can be. You have to see yourself sweeping across a stage or lilting on a ballroom floor. And never take your eye off your dream.

What does that have to do with Santa Claus?

Well, I'm just trying to explain the power of believing. I mean, you believe in me don't you? Do you think an oak tree could talk to a little girl if you didn't believe I could. Well, no. I'd just be standing here with bird poop all over my branches. But the minute you gave me a name and understood that I live and breathe, well, then you could hear my thoughts.

Really?

Really.

But I can't be the first girl you ever talked to.

Well no, but I can talk until my buds burst and no one will hear me if they don't believe. There are maybe a dozen adults in all the land that I can talk to. Poets, mostly. So I spend most of my time with children. But once they turn eight or nine, they think I'm only good for tree houses and lookouts.

But I won't ever stop talking to you, Ollie. You're my best friend. You know everything.

But what about Santa?

Hmmm. That is a little tricky. Wait, I have an idea. Why don't you write him a letter. Think of something you want more than anything. Imagine how great it will make you feel—of all the joy it will bring. If you don't get what you ask for, then maybe Mom is right. But if you do, well then.

That's it! And I won't tell Mom. So it will have to be true if no one knows but me and Santa. You're a genius, Ollie!

Christmas Morning…

What's wrong, Amy. Don't you like your presents?

Oh, I love them Mommy. I was just hoping. Oh, it's nothing really.

But Amy? Oh, was that the doorbell? Who can that be so early in the morning. Amy, slow down.

Daddy, Daddy, you're here. Oh my Daddy!

Surprise! Hi sweetpea.

Jena, my love. I hope those tears mean you're happy to see me.

But you said you wouldn't be home until February.

Well, that's what I thought. But two days ago our commanding officer came in with an early leave for me and about six other guys. Hey, I didn't ask why. I just grabbed my orders and headed home.

Mommy, Mommy. It's true. It's true.

What's true, sweetie?

There is a Santa, Mom. I wrote to him, Daddy. I asked him to bring you home.

Wow. Well, sounds like conclusive proof to me.

Yes, Amy. Yes, I suppose you're right. There is a Santa, after all.

Believe!

A case (in cheek) for why Santa Claus is part Jewish

Point #1: Associated with the origin of Santa Claus are the names Irving and Baum

Point #2: Santa Claus was first created in New York, home to the second largest Jewish population in the world.

Point #3: The modern-day Santa Claus was a product of Macy's and Coca Cola, both very popular among the Jewish population.

Point #4: During the Holiday season all Christians get farchardat.

Point #5: "Gift-giving is not a traditional part of the Chanukkah holiday, but has been added in places where Jews have a lot of contact with Christians." (jewfaq.org)

The Origins of Santa Claus

(Taken from a variety of history sites).

In the British colonies, British (Father Christmas) and Dutch (Sinterklaas) versions of the gift giver merged. In Washington Irving's satirical "History of New York," (1809), Sinterklaas was Americanized into "Santa Claus" but lost his former bishop's apparel, and was at first pictured as a thick-bellied Dutch sailor with a pipe, in a green winter coat.

L. Frank Baum's "The Life and Adventures of Santa Claus," a 1902 children's book, further popularized Santa Claus. Baum gave his "Neclaus" a home in the Laughing Valley of Hohaho, and ten reindeer which could not fly, but leapt in enormous, flight-like bounds. This work also established Claus's motive. When exposed to the misery and poverty of children in the outside world, Santa strived to find a way to bring joy into the lives of all children, and eventually invented toys as a principal means.

In 1926, the Lomen brothers (reindeer herders from Alaska) collaborated with Macy's department stores to stage annual Christmas parades featuring Santa Claus in a sleigh being pulled by reindeer.

The Santa Claus we know today came into being in 1931 for The Coca-Cola Company's Christmas advertising. The massive campaign by Coca-Cola illustrated Santa as he looks today wearing red and white. Coca-Cola and Macy's are largely accredited for having completely removed any remaining remnants of "saint" from "Santa."

Shortly after his Madison Ave debut, Claus met with Rabbi Goldberg of the Reform Congregation of Coney Island. It was at this historic meeting that the tradition of gifts for Chanukkah began. Claus went on to become the CMO of Toys R Us and CFO of the 47th St Diamond Exchange.

Happy Holidays to All !!

Just Believe

Rosemarie Monaco

2009
Heartfelt Wishes

This was a year of transition. In March my father died. In the following months two of my dear friends, Angela and Susan also lost their dads. Losing a parent is life changing for oh so many reasons. I believed that of the three of us, Sue was affected most. Her Dad died young, I believe he was in his 70s, and unexpectedly, and she was especially close to him. She was my inspiration for this story, which also expresses my belief in the power of love.

My story was accompanied by blown-glass heart ornaments.

Just Believe

Rosemarie Monaco

"Hello Cora. Tell me, do you like my Poinsettia? It's really quite comfortable. Very cushy. And red is very flattering to me, don't you think? Cora? What's wrong? Why do you look so sad?"

"My dog Jasper, my very best friend has gone away. My heart is broken."

"Poor Cora. This is a bad time of year to have a broken heart. Not that there's a good time, of course."

"Oh what would you know? Faeries are never blue."

"Well, where on earth did you hear that from? Just because we have wings, and know a trick or two, doesn't mean we are unbreakable. We fight, we cry, we hurt, we ache. Just like humans. The difference is that faeries know the secret remedies to all that ails.

"Faerie dust?"

"Oh, get real. I'm not Tinkerbell and I don't do dust. But I do know all about the heart. And all its secrets."

"I don't think my broken heart will ever mend."

"Come. Let me show you. Here, let your tears fall gently into this jar. Each and every tear is a reflection of your deepest expression of love and tenderness. Go ahead cry your heart out. Now look. Look closely at the jar. What do you see?"

"Oh wow. It's shaped...like a heart!"

"That's because you filled it with so much love. So take it and remember that love stays with you forever. It's the most powerful emotion there is. Do you know that whenever you give love, it comes back to you? Sometimes, in an unexpected way."

"Will Jasper come back?"

"Who can say? But this I know for sure. His love will stay in your heart forever. And every new love you share will keep filling it."

"Like the jar?"

"Yes, just like the jar."

"Take it now. Pass it on to someone else. Give your heart away. Everyday."

2010

Dog Wisdom

I believe this story speaks for itself…

Rosemarie Monaco

Dog Wisdom

Inspiration comes from the most unexpected places…

One day, when I was feeling blue, Zsa Zsa looked into my eyes; she told she loved me and not to worry. I picked her up and hugged her asking for more encouragement. Then, her sister Eva climbed up on my lap. They reminded me of all the wonderful things they taught me…

When love is unconditional,

it's infectious.

You don't have to ask.

If you give love, you'll get lots in return.

You learn from your mistakes.
If you make them again,
you learn some more.
Eventually you get it right
and earn rewards.

We can all get along,
even if we don't always see eye-to-eye.

A walk in the woods
or stroll down the street
should be an adventure.
Filled with discovery.

Playtime is very important.
It refreshes and renews.

Exercise sharpens your wits…
and gives you the stamina
to meet life's challenges (squirrels included).

Don't let your pride get in the way
of asking for what you want.

Howling is good for the soul.
Express yourself.

Be supportive, no matter what.
It sparks courage and strength.

It doesn't matter if you're little.
If you think you are a giant (or a wolf)
you are.

Kiss someone's tears away.
It fixes everything.

Affection is an absolute must.
A hug (or a scratch behind the ear)
is so very healing.

Yesterday and tomorrow don't exist.
There is only now.
Love every minute of your life.

Connecting with another is exhilarating.
Thanks for our connection.

2011

Learning to Fly

Bill, my partner, my love, was the inspiration for this story. We met in January and it didn't take long for us to know that our love was meant to be. He showed me a description of his ideal mate that he'd kept in his wallet for years. It was me. I shared mine with him. We smiled and knew. So I was right! Whatever you can imagine you can create, or maybe in this case, attract.

Life became new, more satisfying. I was me, only better—the me I was meant to be. With no one to hold me back or remind me of my imperfections, I felt free.

I also learned not to regret my past, to forgive the wrongs I had done or were done to me. Because you see, had I not taken a few wrong turns, I might never have found Bill. I was grateful then for choices I had made, for the lessons I had learned.

So, 2011 was the year I learned to fly, to soar, to love who I am deeply and give my love unconditionally. This was the message I wanted to share.

I returned to making my own ornaments. I created a bookmark because books are so inspiring and beautiful examples of bringing your imagination to life. Dangling off the bookmark were charms—bumble bees, wings, gems and hearts.

Just Believe

Rosemarie Monaco

"You've got to find what you love.
And that is as true for your work as it is for your lovers."

–Steve Jobs

I learned to fly today.

What do you mean you learned to fly? People can't fly.

Well who told you that?

No one has to tell me, they just can't. We don't have wings, for one thing.

Oh, well there is your problem right there. You don't need wings to fly.

Are you nuts?

Not at all. Take bumble bees, for example. Their wings are so small in proportion to their bodies, by all the laws of aerodynamics, they should not be able to fly. But they do. Do you know why?

No.

Because they believe they can. They aren't burdened by the laws and attitudes that hold you down.

So what are you saying?

I'm saying that you need to let go of the things that weigh you down, that tether you to the ground.

What things?

Hatred, for one. That's the heaviest. And really, it serves no purpose.

I don't get it.

Well, if you hate someone, that person is unaffected by how you feel, but you are. It fills you up with ugliness. Hatred hurts only the hater.

Hmm. That makes sense. But there has to be more.

Well, if you really want to fly, you also have to forgive. Forgiveness sets you free. It lifts you off the ground. Grudges on the other hand put gaping holes in your wings.

But I thought you said you don't need wings.

The wings are your spirit, your energy, the love that fills you up and lifts you high. Wings are your imagination. Did you know that every dream that comes true starts with a picture?

A picture?

Well, yes. You can see your desires in your mind, right?

Right.

Your dreams set your destination. And love is the rocket fuel.

Close your eyes. Relax and take a deep breath. Go on, try it.

Okay.

Now think of the greatest love you have ever had—for a parent, a child, a lover, a pet, a passion. Focus on that feeling…that wonderful feeling that fills you up and makes your heart swell. Hold on to it. Don't let go. Think of the most beautiful place you have ever been, still holding on to that swelling feeling. See all the beautiful colors and magnificent images that surround you. Can you see?

Oh, my! Oh my! I feel myself lifting off the ground. I understand now. Love makes you fly!

2012

The Butterfly

My friend Angela has written several books about intuition, our God-given key to success. All we have to do is follow our gut. Her books not only teach you how to differentiate your intuition from dream-defying logic, but they are meant to give you the courage to follow your intuition.

This story is about following signs—signs we see every day but ignore, signs that could change your life or someone else's. It's also about seeing the magic those signs hold. When you see the magic, you can't let go, you feel compelled to follow it to its destination. And it is exhilarating. And rewarding.

My story included a beautiful, glittery, red velveteen butterfly.

Just Believe

Rosemarie Monaco

"A sign can take the most unexpected form. Following it can lead to the most unexpected treasure."

-Angela Artemis (author "The Intuition Principle")

Oh my God, Mikey, are you all right? What Happened? Where have you been? It's 9:00 for God's sake. I've been worried sick. Your shirt, it's torn! Tell me what happened.

It's okay, Mom, I'm fine. Really. Nobody hurt me.

Dear Lord, I'm so relieved. But why didn't you get in touch with me?

Well, if I had a cell phone I coulda.

You're eight.

Aww. But let me tell you. Let me tell you. The most amazing thing happened to me.

I'm all ears.

I was having a really bad day. I mean, really. I lost my lunch money. Miranda told me she hated me. I got a D on my report card. So I took the long way home through the footpath in the woods. I was feeling really low. I mean rock bottom. Then suddenly I heard this chirping. A bird, I thought. But then it got louder and louder. Then another bird joined in a little further down the path. At first I ignored it but then another bird started and it was the same sound. It was different than usual. It was weird…as if they were calling to me. The chirping got louder and louder and another one chimed in. Before I knew it there were like six birds all flying toward this tree. Then all of a sudden, they dived down. I thought they hit the tree, but instead they seemed to vanish. Then out of the spot they flew into came this big red butterfly. I couldn't believe my eyes.

Just Believe

Mikey, this is December. There are no butterflies this time of year.

That's what I thought. But there it was. And it had this like sparkly stuff on its wings.

Mikey, maybe it was a Cardinal, one of the birds.

I'm telling you it was a butterfly. You gotta let me finish.

Okay.

So there it was, this red butterfly just flying in circles. Then it came near me then flew away as if it wanted me to follow it. So I did.

And then I saw this little dog with its leash tangled in thorny twigs that were clinging to the tree. It was so helpless. When it saw me, the poor little thing started to cry. I rushed over to it and saw that its little paws were caught in this thorny underbrush. So I helped it out. Good thing I had my army knife on me.

One of its hind legs was all bloody, probably from trying to get out of the bramble. That's when I tore a piece of my shirt to wrap it and stop the bleeding.

I looked at the dog's collar to see if it had an ID tag, but there wasn't any. I looked around thinking maybe it fell while the dog was trying to get free, but nothing.

The dog just curled in my lap as if to thank me. But I figured a dog as friendly as this must have some owners who are really missing him by now. So I decided I would try and find his home.

I didn't know what to do but then I saw the butterfly again. I just knew it wanted me to follow so I did. It stopped at a pond and the little dog was wiggling in my arms, so I let it go and it went straight to drink some water. Lord knows how long it had been stuck by that tree.

The butterfly started circling again. It led me to a big oak tree and it landed on a bunch of acorns. I thought, WOW, maybe this little fellow is hungry. I cracked open the acorns and offered the dog the seed-like stuff inside and he ate it all up.

Next thing I knew it we were way off the path, but I heard the sound of cars ahead so I knew we were near the roadway. I followed the sound. The red butterfly was nowhere in sight. I wandered a bit, hoping I'd see a poster about the missing dog. No luck.

I could see I wasn't far from Main Street and I remembered that the pet shelter was at the end near 9th Street. It was a bit of a walk but I figured that was my best chance at finding the dog's home. When I got there I told them what happened. They looked in their records then said that they had no report of a missing dog like this one so I should just leave it. Some guy came out to take him from me, but something told me this was a mistake. Just as he came to take the dog from me I ran as fast as I could out the door.

Then wouldn't you know it, there it was, the butterfly. I couldn't believe my eyes but I was so happy to see it. It flew in the direction of 7th Street. When we got there I noticed skid marks on the street and at the end of them, near the curb, I saw something shining in the streetlight. It was a dog tag! OMG

I picked it up and went to the address which was about a mile away. When we got to the house, the dog went crazy. I knew it! I knew it was his tag and this was his house. I rang the bell and this lady answered. When she saw the dog, Trixie, turns out he's a girl, she was startled but she immediately let me in her house. She started to cry.

She told me how two days ago, her daughter, Isabel was walking her dog near Main and 7th when she was struck by a speeding car. The dog got tossed they thought and maybe confused and ran in the wrong direction. Isabel was in her bed recovering. She was okay but her mom said she was very depressed and not doing so well because of it. She took me to her.

She was bruised all up. I could see. Trixie jumped up on her bed and Isabel cried and laughed and hugged her. Her mom started crying again. I never saw so much crying.

Isabel smiled at me. Told me I was her hero and that what I had done was so special. Really made me feel good. She hoped we could be forever friends, she said. She's so pretty, Mom. And she goes to my school. She's a year ahead of me.

And Mrs. Stevens, Isabel's mom, handed me some money for bringing Trixie back. I told her I didn't want it, that it was okay, but she insisted.

When I turned around to leave, that's when I saw it, right there on her dresser, a red velvet butterfly with glitter on its wings. Mom, I couldn't believe it.

That is an amazing story, Mikey. I'm so proud of you. Maybe you are ready for your own cell phone.

Wow. Thanks, Mom.

Now about that report card.

2013

The Key

I believe in the Law of Attraction, that your thoughts are creative; and that a positive attitude overpowers that which drags you down. So if you think your life is miserable, it will be and as long as you focus on the misery, it will stay that way. If instead, you focus on what's good about your life, more good things will enter into it. One day my partner, Bill said something that reminded me of this. When the work day gets intolerable, he said, he thinks about me and how good our life together is. Difficult colleagues bother him less and the day gets easier. It wasn't long after that when he got an offer for a new job.

I also thought about "In Pursuit of Happyness," a film based on the life of Chris Gardner, a man who went from being homeless with a young son to care for to becoming a wildly successful stockbroker who could easily provide for his child. It was the quintessential story of focusing on the positive, of visualizing your future and following the road that takes you there. And the results don't always happen immediately, but if you stay focused eventually they will.

I wanted to impart this idea in "The Key" and to let readers know that if they understand that they hold the key to their future, anything is possible. And that you must never give up your dream.

I decorated some shiny skeleton keys and turned them into the ornament for my 2013 story.

Just Believe

Rosemarie Monaco

The Key

Hope was not having a very good day. She seemed melancholy. Her friend, Dillon saw her from across the yard.

"Hey, what's up, Hope?"

"Nothing."

"Well, you look kinda gloomy to me."

"I was thinking about my Mom. I miss her a lot."

"What was she like?"

"She was beautiful. And smart. She used to read to me. She would read from a book then she'd make stuff up about the characters that wasn't even in the book. We'd laugh and laugh."

"Hey, I've got an idea. I know what will cheer you up. Come on with me. There's this place I go to that's just awesome. Come on…I'll take you there."

Dillon led Hope inside to his room.

"This is where you sleep. What's so awesome about this place?"

"Just wait. I'll show you. Sit down over there, against the wall."

Dillon went over to his bed, reached under the pillow and pulled out a big, shiny skeleton key.

"See this? It opens the door to my secret room."

"Really? Where is it."

"Just wait. And I'll show you. Here, hold the key in your hand. Close your eyes. Breathe in deeply. Three times."

"What?"

"Just do what I tell you and you'll see. Now, eyes closed. If you look carefully in front of you you'll see a door."

"I don't see anything."

"Look again. It's a big, wooden door made of thick planks of wood bolted together. It's arched at the top. It has no door knob. Just a keyhole. Can you see it now?"

"Yes, Yes, I can."

"There's a bright light shining through the cracks inviting us to the happiness on the other side. Now take the key, put it into the keyhole and turn it slowly."

Hope reached out but hesitated.

"Here I'll go first. Just follow me close by."

"Okay."

"I'm opening the door now. Come on with me and you'll see the how great it is. There are a ton of big green trees. And a path that leads to a field of purple, blue and pink flowers. We can sit over there under the apple tree. This is not your usual apple tree. When the apples fall down, they splash into a little pool of caramel. Then they roll over onto a bed of coconut. You can have as many as you want and never get sick."

Hope smiled widely. "Over there. Look chocolate bunnies running after the gummy bears!"

"Yeah. I see them too. Oh no. Is that who I think it is? It looks like Mrs.

Weedly," said Dillon referring to their school principal.

"Look at how her ears have grown. And she's got a tail," laughed Hope.

"And a cow bell," added Dillon. "But we gotta be careful," he said through a chorus of giggles. "if she gets mad, she'll turn into the Hulk! Hurry, let's get outa here."

Still laughing, the children ran along the long tree-lined path that led to another opening. It was calm and serene. A swing glided beneath a big oak tree as the soft wind gave it momentum. A pebbled path led to a white house that was studded with green shutters and a matching green door. A porch wrapped around the house. As the children approached the stairs leading to the front door, Dillon pointed to the toys and games that speckled the porch telling tales of happy, unfinished playtimes.

"Should we ring the bell?" asked Hope.

"Don't have to. I've got the key. This is where I live." As Dillon opened the door, a woman greeted them. "Well, where have you been, young man?" she said.

"Mom, this is my friend Hope."

"Hello Hope. So nice to meet you. Come in. Your dad's home."

"Well, hi," welcomed his dad.

"Hello," said Hope, shyly.

"My dad builds bridges and my Mom is a doctor. I come here almost every day to see them."

A loud knock at the door broke the children's spell. Samantha quickly slid under the bed.

"Dillon, we need you to come with us. Dr and Mrs. Hayvn want to meet you. They are very keen on adopting a boy just like you."

Awestruck, Dillon followed the director of the orphanage out the door. Halfway down the hall he said, "Wait, please. I forgot something really important."

Dillon ran back to his room to find Hope sitting in the corner somewhat dumbfounded. "Hope, here, I want you to have this, the key to my secret door. Use it. Use it every day. And you'll find a new mom too. All you have to do is know you have the key and just believe."

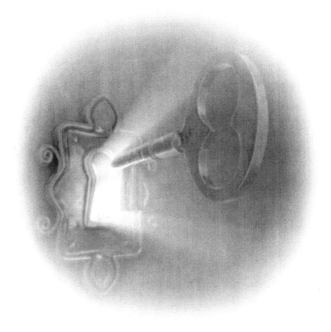

Just Believe

Stories of Inspiration

Rosemarie Monaco

CPSIA information can be obtained at www.ICGtesting.com
Printed in the USA
BVOW02s2152200515

401281BV00007B/16/P

9 781500 883270